LITERALLY DISTURBED

TALES TO KEEP YOU UP AT NIGHT

by Ben H. Winters
illustrated by Adam F. Watkins

This book is for Milly, but not for now. When she's a little older—BW

PRICE STERN SLOAN
Published by the Penguin Group
Penguin Group (USA) Inc., 375 Hudson Street, New York, New York 10014, USA
Penguin Group (Canada), 90 Eglinton Avenue East, Suite 700, Toronto, Ontario M4P 2Y3, Canada
(a division of Pearson Penguin Canada Inc.)
Penguin Books Ltd, 80 Strand, London WC2R 0RL, England
Penguin Ireland, 25 St Stephen's Green, Dublin 2, Ireland (a division of Penguin Books Ltd)
Penguin Group (Australia), 707 Collins Street, Melbourne, Victoria 3008, Australia
(a division of Pearson Australia Group Pty Ltd)
Penguin Books India Pvt Ltd, 11 Community Centre, Panchsheel Park, New Delhi—110 017, India
Penguin Group (NZ), 67 Apollo Drive, Rosedale, Auckland 0632, New Zealand (a division of Pearson New Zealand Ltd)
Penguin Books (South Africa), Rosebank Office Park, 181 Jan Smuts Avenue, Parktown North 2193, South Africa
Penguin China, B7 Jiaming Center, 27 East Third Ring Road North, Chaoyang District, Beijing 100020, China

Penguin Books Ltd, Registered Offices: 80 Strand, London WC2R 0RL, England

Text copyright © 2013 by Penguin Group (USA) Inc. Illustrations copyright © 2013 Adam F. Watkins. All rights reserved. Published by Price
Stern Sloan, a division of Penguin Young Readers Group, 345 Hudson Street, New York, New York 10014. *PSS!* is a registered trademark of
Penguin Group (USA) Inc. Manufactured in China.

Library of Congress Cataloging-in-Publication Data is available.

ISBN 978-0-8431-7194-5   10 9 8 7 6 5 4 3 2 1

LITERALLY DISTURBED

TALES TO KEEP YOU UP AT NIGHT

by Ben H. Winters
illustrated by Adam F. Watkins

PSS!
PRICE STERN SLOAN
An Imprint of Penguin Group (USA) Inc.

SCARY STORIES

You shiver,
your heart going *tap-tappa-tap.*
You quiver
and leap into somebody's lap.

You discover
your mouth's hanging open—yet you can't speak.
You cover
your face with your trembling hands—
then you peek.

The stories sound real.
(At least that's how you feel,
though you know, in your heart, that they ain't.)
You say, "Can't fool me."
"There's no way." "It can't be!"
You stand up, you sit down,
you nearly faint.

But you listen,
to stories of vampires and zombies galore,
to stories of hauntings and murder and gore,
and each one more scary than what came before—
till at last you leap up and race out the door!
Then crack it open
and say, "Hey, I was hopin' you
could maybe just tell me one more?"

BLACK CAT

There's a cat named Raina
at the end of our street,
who's all black with one patch of white hairs.
Just a fuzzy old kitty
with thin yellow eyes,
who sits in her window and stares.

Now, Charlie says Raina's
not really a cat;
Charlie insists she's a witch.
He says that *cat*
is her earthly form,
and if you watch her at midnight
she'll *switch*.

Evelyn says Raina's
not really a cat;
she's a ghost, is what Evelyn swears.
Raina sees visions
from life's other side
when she sits in her window and stares.

Taylor says Raina's
not really a cat;
she's a monster, a man-eating beast.
When Raina sits staring
what she's doing is waiting
for a chance to set off for a feast.

I don't know about any of that.
But I don't get too close to the cat.

WITCHES IN STORIES

Witches in stories catch neighborhood strays
and cackle while dreaming up terrible ways
to mistreat 'em.
Witches in stories fly around on their brooms.
They lure wicked children to gingerbread rooms
and eat 'em.

Witches in stories are skinny and mean.
Their faces are ugly; their skin is all green
and warty.
Witches survive on the souls that they've plundered.
They hide out in forests and live to a hundred
and forty.

They're at their most happy when others are not,
singing off-key while they circle a pot
in slow motion.
Witches in stories like horrible things:
gathering toad's blood and ladybug wings
for a potion.

Mrs. McFleatcher,
our substitute teacher,
is terribly kind.
She is sweet and refined,
and she's pretty and funny and tall,
and her skin is not green, not at all.
Her singing voice is lovely and rich—
each day she leads chorus precisely on pitch—
and yet
I bet
she's a witch.

THE ATTIC

Come on up to the attic.
Come up if you dare.
Climb up the rickety ladder—
come up and see what's there.

A dressmaker's dummy:
no arms and no head.
A locked black trunk,
an old, broken bed.
Something largish and lumpy,
all wrapped up in a rug.
In every corner a spiderweb,
or a mousetrap or roach trap or bug.

And there's the old bike
you loved as a tyke.
The wheels are all bent, and it's rusty.
And here is a box
filled with T-shirts and socks,
all of them moldy and musty.

And it stinks,

and it's dark,

and it's dusty.

And from a shadowy corner is gleaming
a pair of cold, mysterious eyes.
And what is that rustling, whispering noise?
A sound that you can't recognize.

So let's climb back down from the attic.
Let's close the door quickly, and then
we'll bolt the door of the attic,
and never go up there again.

IT'S NOT JUST A COLD

Ah-choo!
Uh-oh.

Ah-CHOO!
Oh no.

Have a seat on my bed, if you would, Mom and Dad.
'Cause I have some news to relate, and it's BAD.
Sick? No, I wish. I'm not sick. I've been CURSED,
and I'm basically DOOMED, and it can't be reversed.

This happened to Rohan, from school, last December.
First sneezing, then *poof*! He's a frog—you remember?

The only faint glimmer of hope that we've got
are swamp grasses grown in some dark, swampy spot,
which we'll harvest at quarter past twelve on the dot,
then mash up with pig hearts we've left out to rot.

This we crush into a powder, then mix in a drink
with bat bile and snake blood and India ink.
Then I'll drink it, roll over, and stand on my head
while you sprinkle candle wax over my bed.
Then we get a chicken and feed it a—Yes?
The doctor?
Well, sure, we can try it, I guess.

THE NOISE

What is that terrible noise,
filling up the night air all around?
It sounds like a beast
getting down to its feast
with a sickening, lip-smacking sound.

What's that unbearable noise?
It sounds like the grinding of bones!
Like the gnashing of jaws
and the tearing of claws
and the dashing of skulls onto stones.

What is that horrible noise?
There's a whole nother part to it now!
It started with *BANG*
and ended with *CLANG!*
In the middle was something like *ow.*

That god-awful noise!
Like the splash of young boys
being tossed in a pot to make stew!
A horrible yelp, voices calling for help—
getting closer and closer and . . . hey.
Just a second, I think that it . . . say.
Am I . . . whoa.
Is it . . . oh.

That noise, I think, has now faded.
We're in luck; something made it disperse.
Listen—try it—
it's suddenly quiet,
and the quiet . . .
the quiet . . .
is *worse.*

A MONSTER CONFESSES

I eat children.
There, I said it.

I'd eat YOU next if I could.
If I saw you on the street,
I'd say, "There goes some children meat!"
And slather you in ketchup, yes, I would.

You eat chicken.
You eat pork.
I'd eat YOU with a knife and fork.
I'd wash you down with some lemonade
or a glass of sweet iced tea.

You go to school, you're four feet tall,
and I'm sure you're very nice and all,
but you're just a talking hamburger to me.

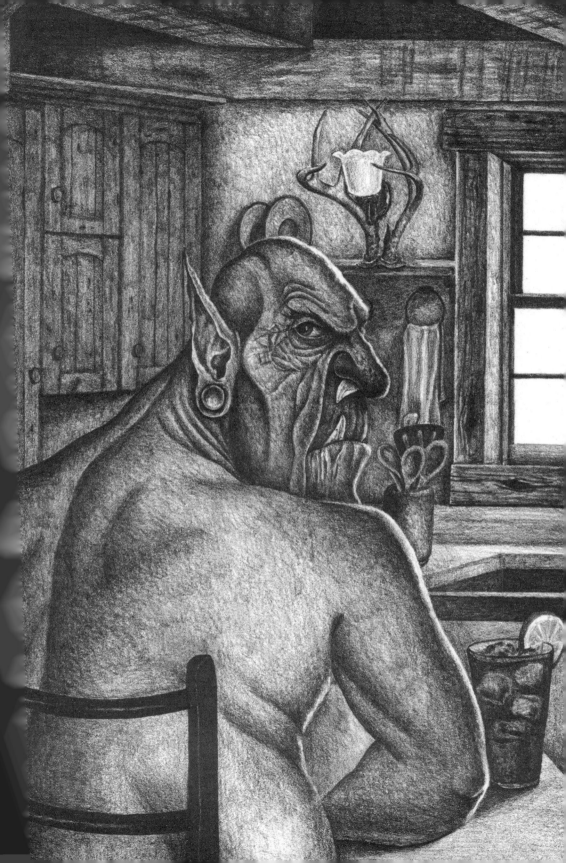

THE SHIP

Out on the sea
*(the deadly sea,
the tossing and terrible sea!)*
there sails a ship,
a PIRATE ship,
with a cap'n as cruel as can be!

Aboard that ship
*(that hideous ship,
that awful, invidious ship!)*
all day ye can hear
the crew shout in fear,
and the snap of the cap'n's long whip!
(I mean it—it's not a nice ship.)

When will they take rest?
When will they find land?
When will they drop their oars in the sand?
The answer, you've guessed it, is *never*!

'Cause they're ghosts, pirate ghosts,
and on they row.
All of 'em drowned ten decades ago,
and they'll be rowing now *forever.*

Out on the sea
*(the endless sea,
the roiling and dangerous sea!)*
there sails a ship,
a lonesome ship,
with the cap'n so mean to his crew.
So, kid, listen up: Live a life good and long,
and if ye think to do wrong,
he's savin' a seat there for YOU.

FULL MOON

Once a month,
the moon gets fat;
the world gets weird.
Imagine that.

Big full moon,
gold and clear,
casts a spell
on us down here.

Some folks cut loose,
play funny games;
twins switch places with their brothers.
Some folks get mean,
fight and call names,
make rude comments to their mothers.

Oh, the moon is strange;
it makes us change—
and some of us change more than others.

THE STATUE

Things have been odd round here lately;
one big, happy family we're *not*
since Daddy got home from the yard sale
and showed off the statue he got:
a monkey with glowing green eyes.

He got it for practically nothing.
"Isn't it gorgeous?" he said.
But Mom didn't find it so charming.
So we stuck it out back, in the shed:
the monkey with glowing green eyes.

Now me and my brothers are fighting;
we argue and bicker and lie.
Mom's moody, and Dad's always quiet,
and I think that I've figured out why:
It's the monkey with glowing green eyes.

On Wednesday I went to bed early—
put my pj's on, got tucked in tight.
And then woke up at three in the morning
in the shed, in the cold, eerie light
of the monkey with glowing green eyes.

So on Thursday it was out with the garbage,
and we smiled as we said our good-byes.
But that night, after we'd had our supper,
just imagine our looks of surprise.
Because somehow, there it was on the mantel—
grinning down at us, wicked and wise—
the monkey with glowing green eyes.
The monkey with glowing green eyes.

WHEN I'M A GHOST

I used to want to be a teacher,
veterinarian, or preacher,
or the guy who tells the weather on TV.

But now what I want to be the most
is a superscary ghost.
I'm serious. That's the job for me.

I'll be grim!
I'll be dreary!
I'll be spooky!
I'll be eerie
when I do my scare-o-rific ghostly dance.
Yes, I'm wanting
to be haunting!
To be mean
and unseen
till I yell "BOO!" and make you pee your pants.

First I'll haunt the kids who giggled
when I fell down in the gym.
And that nasty old bus driver?
Oh yes! Definitely him.

There's only one problem—
it's a big one, I won't lie.
If you're gonna be a ghost,
well, then first you've got to DIE.

SOMEONE'S GOT A VOODOO DOLL

Ow!
Hey!
My leg! My foot! My arm!
Someone's got a voodoo doll, and they want to do me harm!

Ouch!
Whoa!
My butt! My thigh! My neck!
Whoever's got this voodoo doll is jabbing it like heck!

Ah!
Shoot!
My cheek! My chin! My knee!
Each poke at that darn voodoo doll becomes a poke at me!

All right, you all, who's doing this?
Confess, and—ouch! Ooh!
Come on, you brat, stop doing that!
Or I'll make a doll of *you*.

BATS

Creepy things
with leathery wings.

They come out at night
and fly and bite.

They'll swarm around your head—
so be careful if you're tall.
But the *worst* thing about bats?
Some aren't bats at all.

I'M NOT SCARED OF NOTHING

I'm not scared of NOTHING.
I mean it, I tell ya! I'm TOUGH!
I'm not scared of no monsters or spooks,
none of that silly old stuff.

Vampires? Ha!
Zombies? Bah!
I'll invite 'em all over for tea!
To ghosts I say, "Boo,"
to witches, "Pooh-pooh"—
it's THEM who should be frightened of ME.

I'm not scared of NOTHING.
No lizard, piranha, or bug.
Bring me a big, hungry grizzly bear,
and I'll turn him into a rug.

A bully? I'll fight him.
A bulldog? I'll bite him.
I'm fearless—no kidding—it's true!
Tigers? No sweat.
Lions? Don't fret.
I'll show 'em the way to the zoo.

And now it is time for this fearless young soul
to lay down to sleep for the night.
So tuck me in tightly, and please don't forget
to leave on just one little light.

THE DEEP END

You can't see too well underwater.
Everything looks dark.

My cousin's roommate's dentist
was eaten by a shark.

You can't scream underwater,
or say, "Come and help me, please!"
when a tentacle tickles your torso,
grabs you tight, and starts to squeeze.

Most likely there's no danger
here in the lap pool at the Y.

But if you need me,
you will find me
on a beach chair, nice and dry.

A PREDICTION

When he died, he was wrapped up in paper
and stuck in a gold-painted box.
They mumbled some prayers, and they left him
sealed in by a big pile of rocks.

As centuries passed he lay rotting
in his desolate cavern of stones,
in the dullness and dampness and darkness,
with the snakes snaking over his bones.

And his gold got all tarnished and rusty
or was stolen by thieves in a raid.
Then his body was found by explorers
to be dug up and tagged and displayed.

So when, one strange day, he awakens,
I can tell you what he's gonna do:
He'll storm around taking his vengeance—
I mean, come on, wouldn't you?

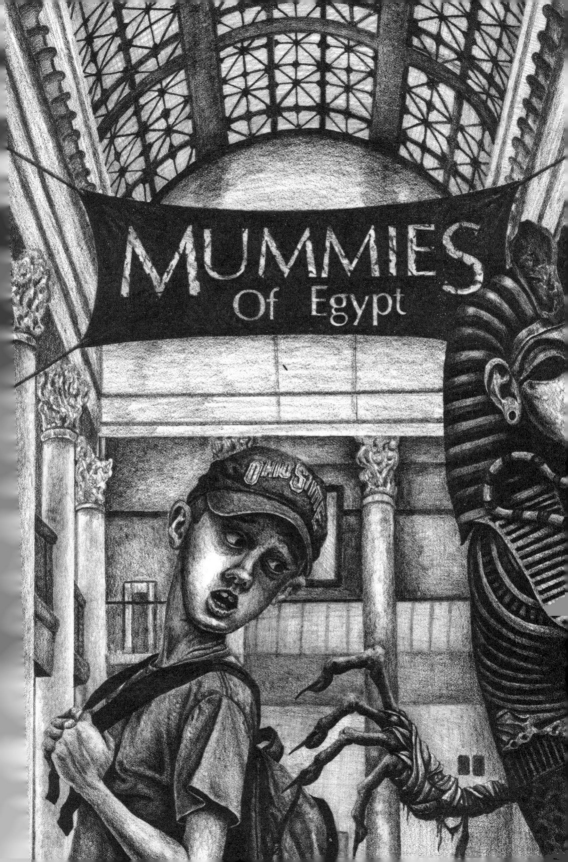

WHAT'S WRONG WITH THE DOG?

"Henrietta, my goodness, what got into you?"
Look how she's howling and trembling, too!
There's no squirrel in the room, there's no cat and no mouse;
there's no danger, no stranger has entered the house.
But she's acting frantic, like never before;
she's pacing and sniffing and pawing the floor.

"What is it, girl? What's got you so thoroughly tweaked?
Why are you acting so totally freaked?
We tell you to *sit* and to *stay*, and you won't.
Oh, what do you see that the rest of us don't?"

POOR THING

We found the poor thing
by the side of the road,
a coughing and pale little sicky.
It was moaning and sighing
as if it were trying
to tell us it felt kind of yicky.

We took it home, the poor thing,
and made it a nest
and gave it a gentle inspection,
while it ate cheese and jam
and most of a ham
and the frog I brought home for dissection.

Look, it's trying to speak!
See it croak through its beak?
I think its big eye is, like, blinking.
It's not pale anymore—
it's more robust than before.
See, it's grunting!
It's moving!
It's thinking!

It's getting well, the poor thing,
so hip, hip, hooray!
Our patient is bigger and stronger each day!
But, um, when it's better, will it go away?

OLD TREE

I look at the tree.
The tree looks at me.

The night is cold.
The tree is old.

Branches and bark.
Moonlight, dark.

Nothing to fear.
Nothing to fear.

Tree's out there.
I'm in here.

HOW I CHECK
FOR MONSTERS
BEFORE I GO TO SLEEP

First I check under the bed,
which is obviously crazy.
A monster that hides beneath the bed
isn't scary—he's just *lazy*.

Next I check the closet,
behind all the pants and shirts.
Make sure I see no beasties
wearing my old skirts.

I turn on the lights in the bathroom,
and once all the shadows are gone
I check that there's no growling fiends
in the tub or on the john.

I glance in the hallway mirror
for a fanged and horrible face.
I look away, then back again—
you know, just in case.

The fridge, the stove, the pantry:
the kitchen is all clear.
I stop and have a cookie.
Why not? Since I'm here.

And then at last I'm confident
that the beasts have stayed away.
Now I lay me down and go to sleep.
Oops—too late—it's day.

OUIJA BOARD

For starters,
we each ask an easy one,
or a silly one,
just for fun.

"Will I pass
science class?"

"Does Principal Flayer
have his real hair?"

You wiggle.
You giggle.

"Will the math exam be hard?"
"Is there gold in our backyard?"

"What's for dinner? Come on, tell!"
"Why does Joshie always smell?"

Josh says, "Hey!"
It's fun. It's play.

Then the lights go out.
You jump. You shout.

In the darkness, someone—who?—
whispers, "Spirit, tell us true!
Go on, tell us, don't you lie,
who of us will be first to die?"

You freeze in place—you're scared to death.
It starts to move—you hold your breath—

ZOMBIES

The zombies are coming!
The zombies are coming!
Run, for the love of God, run!
'Cause they'll eat your brains—
and let me be plain:
That would not be much fun.

The zombies are closer!
They're closer and closer!
Keep moving, people, come *on*!
'Cause they'll eat your brains
till no brain remains—
they'll eat 'em until they're all gone!

Here they come shambling!
Muttering and moaning!
Here they come rambling!
Grunting and groaning!
If you chain 'em they'll just break the chains!
They just keep on coming,
the relentless undead,
and yes—as I said—
they eat BRAINS!

So run, Sally Ann!
Run, Yoko, run, Stan!
Run, Jason, run, Missy, run, Sue!
Run, Rishi and Thomas, and you there—yes, *you*!

They'll gobble up your brains
and his brains and her brains.
They'll eat Margo's and Markie's and mine!

Oh no, one caught me!
It bit me! It got me!
But don't worry, I think that I'm—
BRAIIIIIIIIINS!

WHAT HAPPENED TO LITTLE JAN BANKS?

They say she did it on a dare.
(That's what they say, that's what they say.)
She bragged that she'd go ANYWHERE.
(That's what the children say.)
A nasty kid named Sean McGill
pointed up to Dead Man's Hill.
"Let's see you go up THERE."

She shrugged and said, "Whatever. Sure."
(That's what they say, that's what they say.)
"It's three ten now; I'll be back at four."
(That's what the children say.)
In bright pink sneakers, off she went
up that trail all steep and bent
along the forest floor.

They waited for an hour, then two,
(That's what they say, that's what they say.)
once little Jan was gone from view.
(That's what the children say.)
But Jan, she never did come down,
and soon the whispers raced through town:
The hill had had its way.

What happened next the world knows not!
(Up to this day, this very day!)
Did she get lost, explode, or rot?
(No man alive can say.)
And probably it's all just talk,
poor Jan and her ill-fated walk.
Or maybe it's not.

HEADLESS HORSEMAN

There's a headless horseman on the loose,
riding his mount through the night.
Gathering speed on a terrible steed,
waking the people with fright.

There's a headless horseman on the loose,
but that's not the worst part, doggone it.
'Cause somewhere around,
waiting still to be found,
is the head that has no body on it.

SHADOWS

Shadows make shapes on the wall.
Shadows grow dark on the door.
The shadows spread slowly, they shift and expand,
like wings, they unfold on the floor.

I'm trying to sleep, but how can I?
I crane my neck to see them until it's sore.
The ocean of inky-black shadows
is spreading out on the rug on my floor.

I try to count sheep, but it's useless.
I give up at a hundred and four.
My bed is just one tiny island
in the shadowy sea of the floor.

I stare out the window and tremble.
Oh, how many minutes more?
Before morning arrives with the sunlight
to chase the shadows away from the floor?

THE WITCHES OF EAST McCLINTOCK STREET

Hungaly-mungaly-bungaly-boo.
We're chanting and marching like witches do,
but nothing is happening yet.
We whipped up one heck of a magical potion
from Worcestershire sauce and exfoliating lotion,
which was sadly the best we could get.

'Cause we asked Mama if she had eyes of a frog
and three long hairs from a rabid old dog,
and she said, "I'm afraid I do not."
Nor could we find any tongue of newt.
But we've got string cheese and squeezy fruit,
and we tossed all of that in the pot.

But witches have spells that they carefully learn.
Witches are named Thistle or Fire-Shall-Burn;
we're just Lucy and Marley and Ned.
And really, this bathrobe is makin' me itchy.
I'm tired of marching, and I don't feel too witchy.
How 'bout we go and ride bikes instead?

THE BITE

I just woke in the dark
with a strange little mark
on the side of my neck,
and it itches like heck—
I've been bitten!

Oh, now, here's a surprise
'cause it's *two* marks, like eyes,
and they're swollen and red,
and I'm frozen like lead
where I'm sittin'.

I bet it's still by my bed,
looking down at my head,
its evil eyes staring through me!
This thing that came glidin',
to my room and lay hidin'
until it attacked me
and ate!

I fear this bite was a curse,
which I'll have to reverse,
and I better act fast!
'Cause the night's speeding past!
And I'll soon start to change
to something awful and strange!
I'll be quick! I'll be steady!
Unless it's already
too late.

HIKING

"Come on," my father says. "What's wrong?
You're young, you're fit, your legs are strong,
and we have miles and miles to go!
Get those knees up, why so slow?"

I grimace, and I grasp his hand
and say, "Dad, you don't understand!
I'm not weak; I'm scared, you see,
of what the woods might do to me."

"Oh, dear boy, for heaven's sake—"
says he, but then I see a snake!
And SCREAM! But phew, there's no snake there—
but then I SCREAM! 'Cause, look! A bear!

There's no bear, either. Dad is steamed.
He thinks it's foolish that I screamed.
"You're nuts," he says. "I'm not!" I say.
"And how can you be so blasé?
What if I stumble on a stone?
What if you fall and break a bone?
What if we meet a vampire bat?
What if there're spiders in my hat?"

Dad smiles and says, "Son, just hang on,"
and points . . . And look, the clouds are gone,
and the sun is full and big and bright,
and it casts a warm and golden light,
and there's not a bear or bat in sight.
And the woods don't feel so bad, you know?
"Well, Dad . . . ," I start—Hey, where'd he go?

THE VAMPIRE SLEEPS

In a box, warm and tight,
all day long, like a rat.
Flies out at night
on the wings of a bat.

He alights in your dream
with the fangs and the cape.
You wake and you scream;
it's too late. No escape.

Belly filled, flies away.
Back to his box lined with mud.
Dreams through the day.
And tonight: more new blood.

YOU'RE A SKELETON

You know what you are?
You're a skeleton.
You're a skeleton covered in skin.
I got news for you, friend:
You're a skeleton.
That is just the condition you're in.

You can walk, I know.
You can talk. So?
You can ride a bike, and read a book,
and walk a dog, and tie your shoe.
Beneath it all you're a skeleton.
You are, and I am, too.

Oh yes, yes you are,
you're a skeleton.
You're just bones, at the end of the day.
That's just what we are;
we're all skeletons.
Not saying that's bad, by the way.

If a kid pokes you at school
or says that you're not cool,
makes you sad,
makes you feel small,
just recall:
No matter how smart he is, or tall,
he's nothing but a skeleton,
a bunch of bones, and that is all.

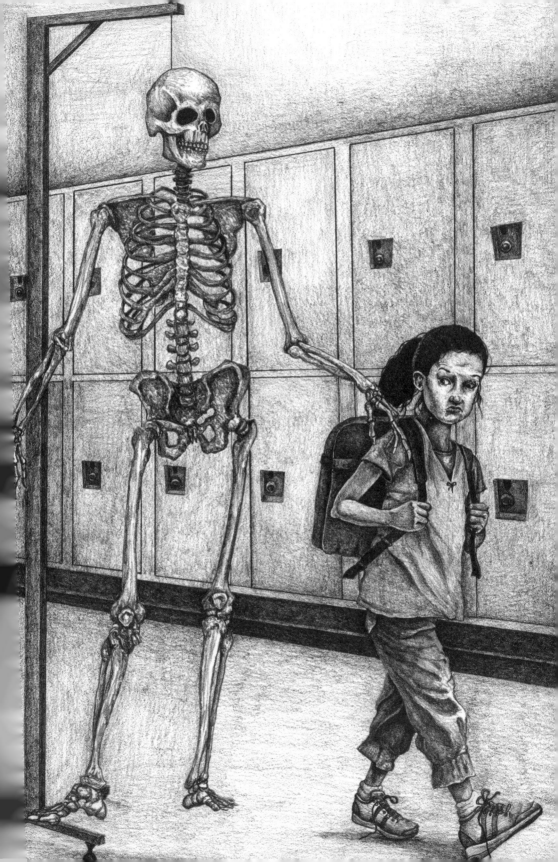